Aziza's Secret Fairy Door

Lola Morayo

Illustrated by
Cory Reid

MACMILLAN CHILDREN'S BOOKS

With special thanks to Tọ́lá Okogwu

Published 2021 by Macmillan Children's Books
an imprint of Pan Macmillan
The Smithson, 6 Briset Street, London EC1M 5NR
EU representative: Macmillan Publishers Ireland Limited,
Mallard Lodge, Lansdowne Village, Dublin 4
Associated companies throughout the world
www.panmacmillan.com

ISBN 978-1-5290-6385-1

Text copyright © Storymix Limited 2021
Illustrations copyright © Cory Reid 2021
Series created by Storymix Limited.
Edited by Jasmine Richards.

1 3 5 7 9 8 6 4 2

A CIP catalogue record for this book is available from the British Library.

Printed and bound by CPI Group (UK) Ltd, Croydon CR0 4YY

MIX
Paper from
responsible sources
FSC® C116313
FSC
www.fsc.org

For Elizabeth and Rebekah.
May you continue to dream big!
T. O.

For Tiger Tamsin.
You are magic in every possible way
J. R.

For Jasmine Richards. Thank you for taking a punt on me
to bring this magical world and all of its characters to life
C. R.

ice mountain

hills

the wailing
woods

police station

lage hall

Zorigami
clockmaker's
workshop

echo
patch

playground

post office

hills

supermarket

village school

Chapter 1

'Bedtime, Zizi!' Mum called from the kitchen.

Lying on her tummy, fingers all sticky with paint, glue and sequins, Aziza was NOT READY for bed.

'But Mum I haven't finished!' Aziza frowned

as she stared down at the wooden fairy door. 'I need to get this sticky gem in *exactly* the right place.' Mum walked into the living room.

'Actually, you need to get those sequins off my rug! Dad only just hoovered!' Aziza

glanced round at the mess. Honestly, it wasn't

that bad, and the sequins sparkled like fairy

jewels on the stripy rug. Besides, Aziza could

hear the smile in her mum's voice. *Maybe she thinks the sequins look like fairy jewels too?*

Mum knelt down. 'Come on, Zizzles, you've been working on that kit all day.'

Aziza sighed. 'I know, but it's been *soooo* fiddly.' She smiled her very best smile. 'Please Mum, just five more minutes? I've almost finished.'

'OK, five minutes tops.' Mum headed out the door. 'Just because it's your birthday, it doesn't mean your bedtime has changed!'

Aziza nodded and then picked up the fairy door. 'Who sent you to me?' she whispered into the quiet of the room. 'Where did you come from?' The door had arrived in the post first thing that morning, but there had been no stamps on the sparkly box. No note. Just her name.

'It's an enormous birthday-sized mystery, Zizzles,' Dad had said when he'd given her the package over breakfast. 'I wish I knew more.'

Aziza rolled her eyes as she remembered his words. *Dad's always playing tricks*, she reminded herself. *He probably got it from the bargain bin in the petrol station.* She shrugged. It didn't matter where the fairy door came from because she LOVED it.

In fact. Aziza loved everything to do with fairies. She'd read all of the Fairy Power series and even had a fairy colouring book and a reversible sequin 'Fairies Rule' T-shirt. Mum was convinced that Aziza's fairy fascination was down to the fact she was named after a type of fairy found in West African folk tales.

She was also named after her Great Aunty Az, who Dad said was always flitting from place to place helping people and making them smile. Aziza had never met Aunty Az but it sounded like she was a real-life fairy making people happy.

Aziza wanted to feel happy looking at the door, but she wished the yellow paint wasn't smudged. She wished there wasn't dried glue on the hinges and that the stick-on jewel for the doorknob wasn't so wonky.

It looks like Kara and Kienan the Craft Power Fairies sneezed all over it. Aziza wrinkled her nose. *Oh, well, at least I finished it.* Aziza picked up the kit's instruction sheet and read through the final part.

Go to your garden,
Put your door by a tree.
Make a wish,
And a fairy you will see.

A GARDEN? Aziza looked around her fourth-floor flat and the door leading to the balcony, which was the closest thing her family had to a garden. Walking over, Aziza peered through the steamed-up glass. There were certainly no trees, but in one corner rested four muddy bikes, and in another a small mountain of broken action figures, most of which belonged to her big brother, Otis. A stack of metal boxes took up what little space remained. They were full of the graphic novels her parents wrote and illustrated about a superhero called Jamal Justice, or JJ to his friends. Aziza smiled as she thought about Jamal and his amazing Ray Atomizer.

'If JJ was actually real, he'd materialize a tree for me just like that,' she whispered to herself. 'Even a plant might do the jo—'

Aziza clapped her hands. *'Glittersticks!'* she cried as an idea popped into her head. Aziza grabbed the fairy door and dashed to her bedroom. She raced past her bed with the fairy duvet, past her bookshelf filled with fairy books and straight to the windowsill. On it sat a perky plant with broad green leaves and a sunny yellow flower. *Okay, a peace lily isn't exactly a tree*, Aziza thought. *But it will have to do.*

'Hey, Lil, would you like some company?'

10

Aziza asked softly. She gently placed the

fairy door next to the plant and crossed her

fingers tight. *Please, please work*, she

wished. *I really would love*

to meet a fairy.

The bedroom
door crashed
open.
Whoa!
That was
quick! Aziza
whipped
round.

It was her brother.

'Oh, it's you,' Aziza said, trying not to sound

too disappointed.

'Hey, Zizi,' Otis replied. 'Have you seen

Captain Bones?'

'You've lost him again?' Aziza shook her head. Her brother was always losing his action figures. 'I haven't seen him.'

Otis's face fell.

'But I'm sure he'll turn up soon,' Aziza reassured him quickly. 'When did you see him last?'

'I was playing with him in the living room.'

Aziza tapped her chin. 'Near the sofa, right?'

'Yeah, why?'

'Well, if you left him near there, I bet Dad knocked him underneath when he was hoovering,' Aziza explained.

'Ah, thanks, sis. That makes perfect sense. Brilliant detective work as usual.' Otis sped out of the door, almost colliding with Dad.

'Slow down, Usain Bolt!' Dad shook his head and walked up to the fairy door. 'Nice work,

Zizzles. You proud of yourself?'

'It's wonky and smudged,' Aziza grumbled.
'I wanted it to be perfect.'

'Really?' Dad replied. 'Can you imagine
how boring the world would be if everyone
or everything was perfect?'

'I guess so.' Aziza bit her lip.

Dad tipped Aziza's chin upwards. 'I
know so. What counts is that you did your
best.'

Aziza thought about that as she brushed
her teeth. She had tried her best when
decorating the fairy door, hoping that if

it was perfect, the magic would work. But it hadn't. No fairy had appeared.

❀ ❀ ❀

That night in bed, Aziza cheered herself up by reading a chapter of the latest Fairy Power book. There was loads of flying in it – loop the loops, deep dives and fay flips. Flying was what Aziza loved most about the stories. Snuggling down sleepily, after her bedtime kiss from Mum and Dad, Aziza hoped she would dream about fairies and zooming through the sky.

She was almost fast asleep when she

heard the knocking sound.

Aziza sat up and rubbed her eyes, just as another knock echoed through the room. She looked at the fairy door.

It was shuddering as if something was banging from the other side.

Aziza padded over to it.

KNOCK. KNOCK. KNOCK.

No way, Aziza thought. *Is the door actually magical?*

Aziza hesitated for a moment, then carefully reached out for the stick-on gem doorknob with her thumb and index finger. Warmth

shot through her hand, up her arm and then through her whole body. She felt like a bottle of fizzy water that had been shaken up.

The door was growing and the shiny doorknob now filled Aziza's whole hand. Even the lily seemed to be getting bigger. Aziza gripped the doorknob tighter as she realized something.

The world around me isn't growing.

I'm SHRINKING!

Aziza stared at the doorknob which looked just like a real jewel now, glittering and bright. With a twist of her wrist and a gentle tug,

the door swung open. A golden beam of light flooded through, bathing Aziza in its warmth.

It felt like an invitation.

Aziza took a deep breath and, with a final glance back at her bedroom, stepped through the doorway.

Chapter 2

Aziza's head was filled with the sound of her heartbeat. It was like a drum that kept speeding up. The golden light faded and she found herself in a sprawling space with a high ceiling, twisting corridors, and lots

of shelves stuffed with . . . toys.

'Whoa!' she breathed.

Each shelf displayed something that Aziza wanted to play with *immediately*. From ginormous teddy bears with friendly smiles to the little towns and cities made of blocks. She spotted some itty-bitty dolls so small that Aziza couldn't imagine anyone playing with them. Not anyone the same size as her anyway.

What is this place? Aziza asked herself. She looked behind her at the fairy door, which glowed brightly next to a stone wall. It was giving nothing away.

A tiny hot-air balloon floated past with an even smaller action figure in the basket. *Hey, was the action figure waving?* Aziza wondered. A train track was laid out on a nearby table and steam engines whizzed around it. Small puffs of steam drifted above the trainset like miniature marshmallow clouds and escaped through one of the room's high windows. In one corner, a towering ballerina made of bronze spun in a slow pirouette atop a music box. She winked at Aziza.

Aziza winked back and stepped towards the giant toy just as something hard and round and very slippery rolled under her foot.

'ARGH!' Aziza's arms windmilled as she lost her balance, but then a strange fluttering feeling spread across her back and she was standing upright again. She glanced over her shoulder. *Glittersticks!* She had *actual* fairy wings. Just like the characters in her Fairy Power books. *Scrap that.* These were far better – they were beautiful orange and black butterfly wings! Her pyjamas had been

replaced by a really pretty dress and, touching

her head, Aziza realized that her silk bedtime

scarf was gone as well.

The fairy door really has changed everything, she marvelled. *But what made me slip?*

Aziza searched the floor and spotted a large blue marble rolling away across the ground. A twinkling light swirled inside it, like a tiny galaxy. *Cool.* Aziza tried to fly over to it, but her wings only gave the littlest flutter. Her feet didn't even leave the floor. *Hmm, so actual proper flying is going to take practice,* she realized. Walking would have to do for now.

Aziza followed the marble a little way down the corridor. As she got closer to it, she heard the sound of arguing and ducked

behind one of the tall shelves. Aziza peeped

out from behind a stack of jigsaw boxes and

saw three fairies, who appeared to be the

same age as her. They were standing around

a huge barrel, glaring at one another. The

barrel had a sign that said,

'You're forgetting, I'm in charge,' said a blue-haired fairy with beetle-type wings that shone green, blue and gold. She crossed her arms. 'That means I get to look in the lucky dip again.'

'That's not fair, Kendra,' the fairy next to her replied. Her pink afro billowed around her face in a pretty riot of springy coils.

'Noon's right,' piped up the third fairy. She had moth wings. 'Why is every turn your turn?'

'Sorry, Felly, I can't really hear anything except an annoying buzzing sound.' Kendra leant into the barrel and began rooting about.

'Hold my legs,' she commanded in a muffled voice.

'I don't see why she can't fly, Lazy Wings,' Felly said, but Noon shrugged and they took hold of Kendra's shiny black boots.

Soon, wooden toy soldiers, glittery keyrings, shiny whistles and blue marbles were being scattered around the room as Kendra dug through the barrel. Aziza spotted a couple of marbles bounce off her fairy door which was still glowing in the far corner of the room. The marbles made a loud thudding sound as they hit the wood.

So that's what was knocking on the door, Aziza thought to herself. She stood up behind the jigsaws. *Come on Aziza. Stop being so shy. Introduce yourself. Sure, Kendra seems a little . . . erm . . . grumpy, but they're real-life fairies and maybe they'll teach you to fly and then you'll be friends and—*

'Why are we even wasting our time with this silly lucky dip?' Felly grumbled. 'There are loads of other things here we should be testing out.'

'You're right,' Noon agreed. 'And we're not even really supposed to be in the store-room, are we? We should get a move on

and take the toys we want.'

Aziza frowned. *Not supposed to be back here in the storeroom*, she repeated to herself. *Take the toys?*

Kendra continued to rummage. More toys pinged around the room.

'She's looking for more charms for that silly bracelet of hers, isn't she,' Felly whispered to Noon. 'It's not like the bracelet is even made out of real moon silver.'

'I heard that!' Kendra snapped. 'Pull me out and get the bags ready.'

Aziza spotted the bulging sacks that were

dumped on the floor. The letters S.W.A.B.
were stitched into the fabric.

S.W.A.B. What did that mean? Aziza

knew swag bags were something robbers
had in books. Was this a similar thing? Aziza

gasped. *Were these fairies stealing?*

'Hey! Stop right there!' Aziza stepped out in front of the fairies. 'It's wrong to take things without permission, you know.'

'Gah!' Felly and Noon jumped in surprise and let go of Kendra. The fairy disappeared into the lucky dip with a squeal.

'Who are you?' Noon asked

'Where did you come from?' Felly added.

'And who put you in charge?' Kendra demanded, emerging from the barrel with a flutter of her wings.

'I'm not in charge.' Aziza lifted her chin.

'I'm just saying that stealing is wrong.'

'Who said we were stealing?' Felly sounded outraged. 'We're just borrowing stuff to test out at home.'

Noon held up a bag. 'See, it's written right here: Stuff We Are Borrowing – S.W.A.B. Mr Bracken won't mind. I mean, if we asked him, I'm sure he wouldn't mind.'

'I'm not sure you should borrow anything without asking first,' Aziza said.

Kendra waved a hand airily. 'Our parents are his best customers. I've even heard my mum say that she's practically bought this place twice over with the amount of money she's spent over the years.'

Aziza felt her cheeks heat up. Maybe these fairies were allowed to borrow this stuff without asking? Maybe that's how things were done around here?

'Hey, don't look so serious,' Noon said.

'Try smiling a bit more,' Felly added.

'Smiles for miles, that's my motto,' Kendra revealed.

'I thought your motto was "Take your paws off that. It's mine!"' Noon looked confused.

Kendra glared at her friend. 'Details, Felly.

Details.' She looked at Aziza. 'What exactly are *you* doing here in the storeroom? Do you live in Shimmerton? I don't recognize—' Kendra broke off. Her eyes went wide. 'Is that a charm?' she breathed. Clutching her S.W.A.B. bag, Kendra fluttered right past Aziza and stopped in front of the fairy door. 'No, it's better than a charm. So pretty. So shiny. So *me*!' Before Aziza could utter a word, Kendra grabbed the bejewelled doorknob and . . . YANKED! It came off completely.

'Nooo . . . !' Aziza gasped as the fairy door juddered violently. Its glow faded in an instant and then the doorway's edge began to seal over, leaving behind a completely flat sheet of wood.

Aziza ran up to the door. She didn't understand everything that was going on or even where she was, but she knew her fairy door did not look like a door any more.

'Put that doorknob back,' she commanded.
'It doesn't belong to you.'

Kendra shrugged. 'Finders keepers, never mind weepers.'

Felly and Noon joined their friend by the door.

'Oh. Actually. That's *definitely* your motto, Kendra,' Felly said.

'You say that "finders keepers" thing the *whole* time!' Noon added.

'Maybe I should put it on a T-shirt?' Kendra mused.

The three friends laughed and it was

a high tinkling sound.

'Guys, it's not a laughing matter,' Aziza said.

'We're the Gigglers,' Kendra replied. 'Laughing is what we do best.'

'Please put the doorknob back.' Aziza tried to keep her voice calm. 'I need it to get home.'

'Make me,' Kendra said, and shoved the doorknob inside her S.W.A.B. bag. With a whirring sound, she beat her shiny wings and flew up towards one of the storeroom's windows.

'Oh no you don't!' Aziza leapt up and

grabbed at Kendra's dangling legs – but missed. Felly and Noon took flight also, their bags over their shoulders.

Aziza tried to flap her wings. She jiggled her shoulders and jumped on the spot.

It didn't work.

Fine. Aziza hopped on to one of the tall shelves and began to climb as quickly as she could. Her arms ached from pulling herself up, but soon she was within reach of Noon.

Gotcha.

She lunged forwards but managed to grab only the outer edge of Noon's S.W.A.B. bag.

The fabric ripped and Aziza tumbled to the ground, landing in the squishy lap of a cuddly toy dragon.

'See you later. Not!' Kendra giggled. With a taunting wave, the Gigglers disappeared through the open window.

Aziza threw the scrap of sack fabric in her hand to the floor. *How am I going to get home without that doorknob?*

Chapter 3

Aziza looked around the storeroom and spotted a heavy metal door in the far corner. Maybe she could find someone to help? Pushing open the door, she walked straight into the toy shop of her dreams!

A doll house sat on a tall display in the centre of the room. Tiny figures dressed like builders weaved in and out of the rooms as they hammered and banged at the walls, adding storeys as they went. In a nearby corner hung an arts and crafts sign with a giant canvas sitting beneath it. Paintbrushes zigzagged across it as if held by invisible hands. As Aziza stepped closer, the brushes sped up and her eyes widened as she realized they had started painting her.

'What were you doing in my storeroom,

young lady?' a voice brayed.

Aziza turned round to see a unicorn, the size of a Shetland pony, behind the shop's counter and she couldn't help but stare. Mum always said it was rude to stare. *But*

it's a unicorn, she thought. *A unicorn in a tank top!*

Aziza opened her mouth to reply, but nothing came out. She had no words (and that hardly EVER happened).

A unicorn is talking to me. An actual unicorn! It has a horn and everything.

Aziza tried to speak again, but still nothing happened.

'Are you okay?' For the first time, Aziza noticed a fairy, who looked like she might be a similar age to her. The fairy was wearing a muddy yellow dress and was looking at her with a worried expression. A pair of feathery wings sprung from her back, so white they almost glowed.

Beside her stood a creature that Aziza didn't recognize at all. Almost as tall as the fairy's shoulder, he was covered from head to toe in light brown fur. They were all staring at Aziza, as if *she* were the odd one out.

'No, I'm not OK,' Aziza said, and she told them the whole story about the fairy door, Kendra, Felly and Noon, the S.W.A.B. bags and the stolen doorknob.

'That's terrible!' cried the fairy in the yellow dress when Aziza had finished.

'Terrible nonsense,' scoffed the unicorn.

'I know those girls you are talking about. They're from Giggleswick Street, a lovely part of town, and you're making them sound awfully naughty.'

'They *are* naughty, and they have my doorknob,' insisted Aziza.

'You must be mistaken,' the unicorn interrupted, 'which is understandable since you're new in town. But those three fairies are the sweetest you'll ever meet. They wouldn't even understand the meaning of bad behaviour.'

The fairy in the yellow dress snorted. 'That's

not true, Mr Bracken. Those three do what they want, when they want. You grown-ups just don't seem to notice.'

'I respectfully disagree, Your Highness.' The unicorn tossed his mane. 'I will check the storeroom. I'm sure there is a perfectly reasonable, grown-up explanation for all of this.'

He trotted past Aziza.

She bit the edge of her thumb. *That didn't go too well*, she thought. *And Kendra, Noon and Felly still have my doorknob. How am I going to get home?*

'Is there anything I can do to cheer you up?' said a gruff voice. 'I'm Tiko by the way.'

Aziza looked down at the bear-like creature who was speaking for the first time. She shook her head.

'And I'm Peri,' the girl added.

'Princess Peri. She's kind of royal,' Tiko announced. 'Her parents are the King and Queen of Shimmerton.'

'A real fairy princess? Do you live in a palace?' asked Aziza.

'Yes, but I don't like palaces.' Peri's face creased into a sudden scowl. 'They're really boring and you have to speak quietly because of all the important meetings.'

Aziza smiled despite herself. That did sound boring. 'I'm Aziza.'

'Sorry the Gigglers took your doorknob,' Peri said. 'But if you truly can't get home without it, Shimmerton's not a bad place to be stuck forever.'

FOREVER? Aziza sniffed hard, trying

to hold back tears.

Tiko shot Peri a warning look.

'I'm sorry, I didn't mean to make you sad,' Peri said quickly. 'My mother says I shouldn't just blurt things out. My mouth is faster than my brain sometimes.'

'It's OK.' Aziza rubbed at her eyes. 'The same thing happened with those Gigglers. I asked if they should really be taking stuff without asking. I think I upset them, but I couldn't help it. It seemed wrong what they were doing.'

Tiko nodded in agreement. 'It is wrong.

I don't think they understand how naughty they are sometimes. Nobody ever says 'no' to them, you see. Oh well.'

'What do you mean, oh well?' Aziza's tears were quickly disappearing.

Tiko's little nose began to twitch. 'Um,' he began. 'There's nothing we can do . . . is there? They always get away with stuff like this.'

Aziza narrowed her eyes. 'Of course there is! Where is your sense of justice?'

'Justice?' Peri repeated in puzzlement.

'Yes, it's what superheroes strive for. Putting right what's gone wrong.' Aziza tapped her chin. 'At least, that's what Jamal Justice does.'

Peri leant forward. 'Who's Jamal Justice? What's a superhero?'

Aziza gasped. 'You don't know what a superhero is?'

Tiko and Peri shook their heads.

'Don't worry, I'll explain. I'm a bit of an expert because my parents write superhero stories. They do the drawings as well.'

Aziza told them everything she knew about superheroes and gave Jamal Justice the starring role.

'Whoa, I'd much rather be a superhero

than a fairy princess!' Peri exclaimed.

'Princessing is literally the most boring thing

ever. I'm always having to go to boring dinners with folk from different parts of the kingdom. And there are never any other kids there.'

'There's no reason you can't be a fairy princess *and* a superhero,' Aziza said. 'You too, Tiko. You can be a superhero and a . . . bear.'

'I'm not a bear, I'm a—'

'What are we waiting for?' Peri asked excitedly. 'Let's find those Gigglers and get your doorknob back.'

'Really?' Aziza asked.

'Really,' Peri replied. She turned to Tiko.

'You'll come too, won't you?'

Tiko's nose twitched and Aziza realized he did this whenever he was nervous. She held her breath.

'Of course I'll come,' Tiko said.

'OK. We'd better go and find those Gigglers before the trail goes cold,' Aziza said.

'What about Mr Bracken?' Tiko asked.

'Don't worry, I've left him a note.' Peri pointed to a piece of paper.

'Wow, that was quick!' Aziza said. 'Did you use magic?'

'No, a pen and some phonics. Come on,

let's go!'

Chapter 4

'How are we going to find the Gigglers?'
Tiko asked as they spilled out onto a cobbled
street.

'We need to look out for clues. That's what
Jamal Justice would . . .' Aziza trailed off as

she took in Shimmerton properly for the first time. 'Oh wow!' she gasped.

The sun blazed down from a pink, candy-floss-coloured sky filled with spiral-shaped clouds. A row of jewel-coloured shops lined the wide high street which was filled with bustling creatures of all shapes and sizes. A gnome and then a centaur bowed to Peri as they passed by. A little green goblin with a cheeky smile tried bowing too, but it was tricky because she was bouncing along on a candy-cane pogo stick.

It's nothing like the grey high street at home,
Aziza thought. Everything here glimmered
like it had been sprinkled with gold dust.

An amazing humming sound filled the

air with high and low notes. 'What's that beautiful music?' Aziza asked.

'Oh, that'll be the orchestra.' Peri nodded towards a wooden bandstand filled with swaying flowers. 'They're practising for the summer concert.'

'But how are they making the music?' Aziza went over to the green to have a better look. 'Ahh, the petals and stems are vibrating to make that lovely sound!'

'Watch your step there.' Peri put a hand on Aziza's shoulder. 'You're about to walk on a leap stone.'

Aziza looked down. One of the cobbles

shimmered more brightly than the others.

What's a leap stone?

Just then, the goblin on the pogo stick

landed on the sparkling stone and shot straight
up into the air with a happy squeal.

'*Oh my wings!* That's got to be a new leap
record,' Peri said as the goblin sailed across the sky.

Aziza stepped carefully over the leap stone

but then spotted something even more exciting

than a leap stone or musical flowers.

'Wait!' she shouted and stopped dead.

Peri crashed straight into her. 'Ow! My

nose!' she said rubbing her face.

'Sorry about that,' said Aziza, 'but look!' She pointed to a trail of blue marbles on the ground. 'It's a clue. Those marbles must have fallen out of their sacks.'

'So, if we follow the marbles, maybe they'll lead us straight to the Gigglers?' Tiko suggested.

'Exactly,' Aziza agreed.

Tiko smiled shyly.

'Let's go find ourselves some Gigglers!' Peri exclaimed.

They set off at once, and with each marble

they found, Aziza made a new discovery about Shimmerton. Outside the vet's, she saw an ogre carefully cradling a pet porcupine. Peri explained that porcupines were the pet of choice for ogres because the quills discouraged over-enthusiastic squeezing. Then at the local cafe, the dining tables whirled like a spinning teacup ride.

Aziza smelt the bakery before she saw it. The air was filled with the delicious scent of vanilla, cinnamon and baking bread. Her mouth watered. Then she saw the bakery's shop window. It was crammed full of baked goods, but the tarts looked like cabbages, the cookies were shaped like Brussels sprouts and the giant cake looked like a bowl of salad.

Aziza was about to ask about the unlikely looking goodies, when she spotted the distinctive, metallic sheen of beetle wings. *Kendra!*

Ahead, away from the bustle of the high street, was a stone bridge which arched over a wide river. On the other side were three Gigglers, huddled around their S.W.A.B. bags.

'Oi! You three!' Aziza cried running up to the bridge. The Gigglers turned at the sound of her voice.

'Oh, not you again,' Kendra groaned. 'Can't you go make some friends and leave us alone?'

'She's already got friends,' Peri said, arriving at Aziza's side.

'She's got us.' Tiko tried to stand as tall as he could.

Aziza crossed her arms. 'Please give back my doorknob. I can't get home without it. You don't want me to be stuck here, do you?'

'Why would you be stuck?' Noon piped up, looking confused.

'I don't really care. It's pretty and I found it, so it's my doorknob now. And why would you want to be anywhere but Shimmerton anyway?' Kendra wrinkled her nose.

'I love my city, it's where I live with my family and where I go to school,' Aziza said proudly. 'All my friends are there.'

'I like school.' Noon smiled. 'We learn about all the different parts of the kingdom outside of Shimmerton.'

'And the history of magic,' Felly added.

'Can you do real magic then?' Aziza asked, curious despite herself.

Felly shook her head. 'We'll get our wands when we're older.'

'Stop talking to her, Felly,' Kendra interrupted. She scowled at Aziza. 'If your home is so cool, why don't you just go back there?'

'Because you have the doorknob.' Aziza tried to remain calm. 'I've already told you. I need it to get home.'

'Can't you just fly back without it?' Kendra suggested.

'I don't think it works like that. And anyway, I don't even know how to fly.' Aziza could hardly get the words past her gritted teeth. 'I've never had wings before.'

Kendra raised her eyebrows. 'Wow, that's got to be *super* annoying. I bet you really want to fly over this river and come and get this, don't you?' She waved the doorknob at Aziza.

'Stop teasing,
Kendra,' Peri
said. 'Give the
doorknob
back and then
give those toys
back as well.'

'Of course, Your Highness. Straight
away.' Kendra looked very sorry.

Felly and Noon smirked at each other.

'Really?' Aziza's shoulders sagged with
relief.

'Sure thing,' Kendra said. 'Why don't you cross the bridge and come get what's yours?'

Tiko touched Aziza's arm, his nose twitching fiercely. 'Erm, I don't think that's a good idea.'

'He's right. They're always playing tricks,' Peri warned. 'Never trust a Giggler.'

'We can hear you, you know,' Felly called out.

'I'm sure it's OK,' Aziza replied. 'They know how important the doorknob is now.'

Peri gave Tiko a look.

He shrugged. 'Maybe Aziza's right.'

Aziza stepped on to the bridge and jogged over towards the Gigglers.

'Hey,' Kendra called out, just as Aziza reached the middle of the bridge. 'I've got an extra special surprise for you.' She reached into the S.W.A.B. bag and pulled out a tub of purple goo.

'What's that?' Aziza asked.

'Bunyip sludge,' Tiko cried. 'RUN!'

Chapter 5

Aziza dived forwards, just as a blob of slime whizzed past her ear and hit the bridge with a *SPLAT*.

'Nice dodge,' Peri shouted. 'Keep moving!'

Aziza looked over at Kendra to see more blobs

heading straight at her. She tucked and rolled.

Peri zoomed up into the air. 'Right. You guys leave Aziza alone.'

'It's just a bit of fun, Peri!' Felly yelled back. She had her own tub of slime and chucked some of it at the princess. Peri dodged the splat but was driven back to the riverbank as Noon sent more blobs of slime her way.

Glittersticks! I can't believe I thought the Gigglers would actually help me, Aziza thought as the slime hit the bridge, covering it in a thick layer of goo. *But they can't stop me.* She jumped up, cartwheeled out of the way of yet

another blob and dashed forwards. 'That's my doorknob!' she cried. 'And you're going to give it ba—'

Her foot hit a patch of goo, sending her round in a perfect spin. Landing on her bottom, she slid back down the bridge. Aziza came to a stop right next to a ball of fur with big wide eyes that blinked at her.

Aziza blinked back. 'Tiko?'

With a twitch of his nose, Tiko unfurled himself to his normal size. 'I *really* hate slime. It's impossible to get out of my fur.' He checked himself over. 'Plus, my mum hates mess.'

'It's alright, I've got this.' Aziza took a deep breath, then sprinted back up the bridge. Her legs immediately skidded out from beneath her and she slid backwards again. The Gigglers' laughter followed her.

'Thanks for the show,' Noon cackled.

'And your doorknob,' Felly cooed.

With a smug grin, Kendra flew up into the air. 'Wish we could stay, but we've got some unfinished business and it's almost dinner time.' They zoomed off.

Peri fluttered downwards. 'Well, that went brilliantly.' She landed next to Aziza and Tiko.

'I did warn you not to trust the Gigglers.'

Tiko gave Peri a warning glare and the princess fell silent.

Aziza stared at the slime-covered bridge. 'They're never going to give that doorknob back, are they?' Tears filled her eyes.

'Don't worry,' Tiko said. 'We'll find a way. I'm sure we will.'

'By my whiskers! What is going on here?'
asked a squeaky voice. Aziza turned to see
a rather cute bunny . . . with a horn and a
shopping trolley.

'Oh hi, Mrs Sayeed,' Tiko said.

'Hi? What happened to the bridge? I've

got groceries to get home and a baby to feed. We Almiraj might be small but we have big appetites.'

'It wasn't our fault, Mrs Sayeed.' Peri quickly explained about the Gigglers and the sludge.

'Princess Peri, those lovely young ladies would never do such a thing,' Mrs Sayeed said with a shake of her head. 'It has got to be one big misunderstanding.'

'But Mrs Sayeed—' said Tiko.

'I'm sure it was all just an accident and now they've gone to get help,' Mrs Sayeed interrupted. She took another look at the gloopy bridge and sighed. 'I'll have to take the long way round to get to the other side. I hope my carrot ice cream doesn't melt.'

Mrs Sayeed began to pull her shopping trolley along the riverbank. 'I'll be sure to let an Elf and Safety Officer know about the bridge so they can get this cleaned up.'

'Why doesn't anyone ever believe us about the Gigglers?' Aziza asked.

Tiko shrugged. 'They're always super nice to the grown-ups, so they always get away with stuff.'

Aziza looked at the other side of the bank.

'We'll never catch up with the Gigglers if we go the long way round.'

'I could shape-shift into a Kushtaka,' Tiko offered. 'Then you could cross the river on my back.'

'You can shape-shift?' Aziza asked.

Tiko nodded shyly.

'That's amazing!' Aziza exclaimed. 'Um . . . but what actually is a Kushtaka?'

Tiko looked surprised that she didn't know. 'OK, it has short webbed feet and a long, strong tail that's really great for swimming.'

'So, like an otter?' Aziza said.

'Yeah but a bit bigger and a bit more magical,' Peri explained. She hovered up into the sky. 'Do your thing, Tiko, and I'll meet you on the other side of the river.'

Tiko nodded, shut his eyes and scrunched up his face as he concentrated.

Nothing happened.

Tiko cracked one eye open. 'Am I transformed?' He looked down at his body. 'Oh, furballs, I thought I had it this time!' He rubbed his hands and jumped on the spot. 'OK, I'll keep trying. Give me a sec.'

Peri flew back down, landing beside Aziza.

'Listen, whilst he's working on the shape-shifting, why don't I teach you how to fly?'

Aziza poked at the grassy bank with her shoe. 'There's no point. I'm rubbish at flying.'

Peri shrugged. 'That's not true. You just need a little practice.'

'You think?' Aziza started to smile. 'I would love to learn.'

'First rule of flying — it's all about your shoulders,' Peri said. 'Keep your arms by your side but move your shoulders up and down.'

'Like this?' Aziza replied, with a few big shrugs.

Peri cocked her head to one side and watched carefully. 'A bit more to the left,

now to the right. That's it.'

Aziza grinned. 'What next?'

'Now the hard bit. Let go of all your worries,' Peri said. 'They are just weighing you down. Think about how good it would feel to be flying right now.'

Aziza closed her eyes. She tried to let go of her anxiety about the Gigglers and the doorknob. She tried to let go of her nervousness that she might not be able to fly. She began to feel lighter.

'Good,' Peri said. 'Let that positive energy spread across your whole body, right to the

tips of your wings. You should start to feel a little warm.'

Suddenly, Aziza felt her feet leave the ground. *Whoa!* Then up she shot through the air as her wings flapped behind her.

'That's it, Aziza,' Peri called from down below. 'You're flying. I knew you could! Go on! Go faster. Go higher!'

Aziza waved at Peri and Tiko as she did a loop in the sky and then she soared higher still. It felt amazing to feel the wind sting her cheeks. From up here Aziza could see all of Shimmerton laid out before her. There were even more shops on this side of the river and, further out, there were grassy hills filled with flowers. Houses of every shape and size nestled next to a patchwork of streams or under the cover of

tall swaying trees. It was all so beautiful
and peaceful.

Just then Aziza spied some tiny blue objects

catching the light and glinting on the ground.

Wait? I'm sure those are some of the blue marbles

on the grass over there, Aziza thought.

All of a sudden she remembered the need to get the doorknob back, or she would never get home. The thought of that was so heavy in her mind that Aziza felt herself starting to drop like a stone. She tried moving her shoulders but still she plummeted.

'Ha ha! Stop messing about – flapping like a chicken,' Peri yelled up at her.

'I'm not messing about,' Aziza cried. 'My wings aren't working! Help!'

Chapter 6

Peri froze, her eyes wide. She didn't look like
a fairy with a plan.

'Don't worry, Aziza.' Tiko raised his arms
above his head. 'I'll catch you.' Tiko looked
determined.

'OK, Tiko!' Aziza cried and scrunched

herself up into a ball. At the last moment,

he leapt up and caught her neatly, before

gently placing Aziza on her feet.

Aziza gulped, knowing that she would have gone splat without his help. 'Great catch, Tiko. Thank you!'

Tiko smiled and Aziza was sure he was blushing under his fur.

Peri fluttered over to Aziza. 'I'm so sorry. I completely froze. I shouldn't have told you to go higher. Flying is tricky even if you're experienced.'

'Don't worry about it, Peri. It was my choice to go higher as well,' Aziza said. 'But I don't think I'll be flying again anytime soon.

It's safer on the ground.' Aziza shuddered. 'You should go ahead. You can fly, so you'll be much faster than me, and then you can follow the marble trail I saw on the other side.'

'She's right,' Tiko said. 'It's down to you, Peri.'

'Don't be silly,' Peri replied. 'We're a team. We'll solve this together.' Peri put her hands on her hips. 'Soooo, how about I carry you both to the highest point of the bridge and let you slide down to the other side?'

'Um.' Aziza looked down at herself and then at Tiko. 'Don't you think we might be a bit heavy?'

'I'm sure it will be fine,' Peri said, rolling up her sleeves. 'Sometimes, you've just got to give things a go.'

Tiko's nose began to twitch. 'Peri, you promised you'd start being more realistic after what happened on Ice Moun—'

'No, she's right, Tiko,' Aziza broke in. 'Sometimes you *have* got to give things a go. I can try flying again. If I'm careful and we work together, I think we can carry you up the bridge.'

'My lovely clean fur.' Tiko sighed. 'It's time to get messy.'

Aziza grabbed one of his hands and Peri grabbed the other. Using their wings and a lot of determination they half carried and half pulled Tiko up to the middle of the bridge. Then he curled into a little ball and rolled all the way down the other side with a great big, '*Wheeeeeee!*'

Aziza led the way and pointed to where she had seen the marbles. The three of them followed the clues onto a cobbled path. Then the trail stopped.

Aziza looked up.

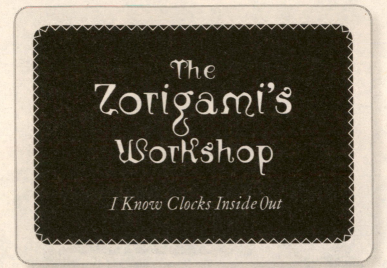

The Zorigami's Workshop

I Know Clocks Inside Out

'What is this place?' Aziza asked.

'The clockmaker's workshop,' Peri said.

'You don't think the Gigglers are in there do you?' Tiko asked. 'That's very brave of them.'

'Brave? Why?' Aziza asked. 'What's a Zorigami?'

'Once a clock survives more than a thousand years it becomes a real life creature called a Zorigami,' Peri explained.

'And they are very stubborn and grumpy,' Tiko added. 'You'd be too if you were a thousand years old.'

'Well, the trail of marbles stops here.' Aziza said. 'The Gigglers must be inside.' She knocked firmly on the door.

It swung open and Aziza tried not to gape at the creature in front of her. It was a clock, but it was also a person.

'We're closed,' the Zorigami tick-tocked.

'We just need to know if you've seen the Gigglers?' Aziza asked. 'It's really important.'

The Zorigami bustled past them, a watering can looped over his arm.

'Those lovely girls? They dropped by a little while ago. Or was it a long time ago?' He shrugged. 'Time means little to me.' The Zorigami watered a flowerbed filled with dandelion clocks. His wooden skin shone in the sunlight.

'What did they want?' Aziza questioned.

'They wanted to borrow some string and other bits and pieces for a craft project. All very hush-hush,' the Zorigami replied.

'Did you give it to them?' Peri demanded.

'Why wouldn't I?' the Zorigami snapped back. 'They had a quick rummage in my workroom and then they left. If you could leave as well, and give this old timepiece a bit of peace please.'

Aziza stepped back on to the cobble path with Peri and Tiko. 'Those Gigglers are up to something,' she whispered. 'I bet they're still in there. There are no more marbles leading away from here.'

Peri nodded. 'You're right, they must be

inside, but how do we get in?'

'I could try shape-shifting again?' Tiko replied.

'Into what? Peri asked.

'A mouse? I could squeeze under the door and have a quick look around. That way we'll know for sure.' Tiko shut his eyes and scrunched up his face again.

Aziza held her breath.

Tiko began to shake then disappeared in a flash of sparkles. In his place was a tiny mouse. Its bright red fur was alive with flames and tendrils of smoke drifted from its whiskers.

'Oh no,' breathed Peri. 'That doesn't look right.'

'*FIRE RAT!*' screamed the Zorigami,

spotting Tiko from his garden. 'Vermin! I won't have it near all my wooden clocks.'

Before anyone could move, the Zorigami ran to them and dumped his watering can over Tiko's blazing head.

Chapter 7

'*Brrrrr*. Chilly,' Tiko said returning to his usual form and wiping water from his face. He looked sheepish. 'I'm really sorry. I didn't mean to turn into a fire rat.'

'It's OK,' Peri assured him gently. 'You

actually shape-shifted this time.'

'Yeah, you're getting better at it,' Aziza added.

The Zorigami frowned, lowering the watering can. 'If that's him getting better, I'd hate to see what he was like *before*.'

'That's not fair,' Peri replied.

'Fair?' the Zorigami tick-tocked. 'He turned into a creature that could have burned down my workshop! Never seen anything like it. Not in all my years.' He shuffled off inside and slammed the door behind him.

Tiko's shoulders sagged. 'What do we do now?'

'Let's wait them out,' Aziza replied, trying to sound confident. 'The Gigglers will have to come out eventually.'

'Well . . .' Peri began carefully.

Aziza frowned. 'What?'

'I hate to say it,' Peri replied. 'But what if they're not in there at all? What if they repaired the sack? The Zorigami said they borrowed some string.'

Aziza swallowed hard. Peri was right. If they have mended the sack, that will mean no more marble trail. No more clues. And no fairy doorknob. Her eyes began to sting with tears. 'I'm never going home, am I?' she finally whispered.

'You could come home with me,' Tiko offered. 'We've got room and my parents love company. Right, Peri?'

But Peri wasn't listening. She had a thoughtful look on her face.

'I think we've been going about this the wrong way,' she finally said.

Aziza frowned. 'What do you mean?'

'Well, we've been chasing the Gigglers this whole time,' Peri said slowly. 'Maybe we need to find a way to get them to come to us instead.'

Aziza raised an eyebrow. 'It sounds like you've got a plan.'

'Yeah, and it's pretty perfect, even if I do say so myself!' Peri replied. 'We can set a trap using all the marbles we've collected. If we pile them up somewhere, the Gigglers won't be able to resist borrowing them.'

'Then we can get the doorknob back,' Aziza finished excitedly.

'Exactly, we just need to . . .' Peri trailed off.

'What's wrong?' Aziza asked

Peri peered around. 'Erm, I'm not sure where we should put the marbles or how the Gigglers will know the marbles are even there.' She scratched her head. 'My perfect plan is not actually that perfect.'

'Um . . . I think I have an idea.' Tiko shuffled his feet. 'But I'm not sure it will work.'

Aziza nudged Tiko with her shoulder. 'I'd really like to hear it,' she said gently.

'We're a team, remember?'

Tiko nodded slowly. 'You see, I spotted an echo patch nearby. If we put the marbles there, the Gigglers will hear us talking about them.'

Peri clapped her hands with glee. 'Oh, that's perfect, Tiko.'

Aziza frowned in confusion 'What's an echo patch?'

'It's an area of upside-down toadstools,' Peri replied. 'They make everything louder, so if the Gigglers are still in the workshop, they'll hear.'

Tiko led Aziza and Peri to the echo patch

and they emptied their pockets of the marbles.

'These marbles are just *so* shiny and pretty!'

Aziza exclaimed. She jumped as the sound

of her voice boomed across the echo patch.

'I can't believe the Gigglers dropped them.'

Peri grinned. 'Yeah, finders keepers. We're going to have so much fun.'

'What game shall we play?' thundered Tiko. 'How about—'

'What's going on here?' boomed a deep voice. Aziza turned to see a tall elf, dressed in a yellow, high-visibility jacket.

His pointy ears peeked out from under a matching yellow hard hat.

'Oh, hello Officer Alf.' Peri's voice was very loud. 'We're just playing marbles.'

'Officer?' whispered Aziza to Tiko.

'Yep. He's the Elf and Safety Officer,' Tiko whispered back.

'Hmm . . . marbles you say,' he replied, his brow furrowed. 'Can I have a closer look please?'

Peri handed him the marble in her hand. 'Here you go.'

Officer Alf walked over to where the light

was a little better. He then peered into the

blue ball, before straightening up sharply.

'I thought as much,' he said. 'I'm sorry,

Your Highness. I will have to confiscate this

marble – and all the others.'

'No!' said Peri, Aziza and Tiko. They ran to

Officer Alf's side. 'You can't. We need it. You

don't understand.'

'I'm afraid I have no choice. This is a

mind-meld marble,' Officer Alf replied with a

sniff. 'A very dangerous thing, and I don't like

dangerous things.'

Aziza bit her lip. 'Are you sure? It looks

just like a regular marble.'

Officer Alf extended

the marble towards

Aziza. 'See that

twinkling light

inside?'

'Yes, it's so

pretty,' Aziza replied

as she examined the marble in his open palm.

The Elf and Safety Officer snapped his

hand shut. 'It's pretty dangerous you mean,'

Officer Alf muttered. 'That light can damage

your eyes, especially as you're supposed

to concentrate on it when you control the marble with your mind.'

'Control it with your mind? Cool,' Peri breathed.

Officer Alf snorted. 'Cool, is it, to accidently transport a marble up your nose or into your ear? Because that's what happens, if you're not careful.' He shook his head. 'These marbles are a menace. I've seen many a broken window because people don't mind-meld with them properly and lose control.' He looked down sternly at the trio. 'Where is this marble from?'

'The toy shop,' replied Aziza. 'The Gigglers

borrowed it and lots of other toys. They also took my doorknob, and I need it to get home.'

'We're on a special mission to help Aziza get it back,' Tiko added.

'And you're kind of ruining it!' said Peri.

'I've never ruined a special mission in my life.' Officer Alf sounded outraged.

'Then please don't take the marbles,' Peri pleaded. 'We need them to lure the Gigglers out of hiding.'

Officer Alf wagged an official-looking finger at them. 'These marbles are much too dangerous and—'

'You don't like dangerous things,' Peri finished with a groan. 'We know.'

Aziza bit the edge of her thumb. This was a disaster – the plan was falling apart. She froze as she heard the very loud snap of a twig and even louder giggles.

She spun around to find the Gigglers right next to the pile of marbles, which they were quietly tossing into Kendra's S.W.A.B. bag, while Peri and the Elf and Safety officer had been deep in conversation.

'Stop!' Aziza cried. But it was too late. The pile of marbles had already gone.

Felly and Noon immediately took flight. Kendra winked, then she shot up after her friends, her wings whirring loudly.

Aziza watched as they sped away. She knew had to try to stop them.

Chapter 8

Let the positive energy flow.

Peri's words filled Aziza's mind, and before she knew it, Aziza was shooting up through the air, right behind the Gigglers. By now, Kendra had caught up to Felly and

Noon and was leading the way.

How did she get so fast? Aziza thought as she tried to keep up with them. Kendra's wings were flapping so fast they were just a blur and they gave off a whirring sound. *There's something different about those wings.*

Then Aziza spotted the metal cogs and wheels that spun at the base of Kendra's wings.

'That must be why they were in the clock workshop,' Aziza whispered to herself. The clockwork was making her faster. Aziza checked and saw that Noon's S.W.A.B. bag had been repaired just as Peri had guessed.

Aziza looked back towards the echo patch. Peri was still talking to Officer Alf, and Tiko was desperately trying to get Peri's attention while pointing up at the sky at Aziza and the Gigglers. When she finally looked up and spotted Aziza, Peri gave her an encouraging thumbs up.

She wants me to keep going, Aziza realized with a gulp. *But what if I mess up flying again?*

Aziza looked back towards the Gigglers. They were ahead of her and picking up speed. She suddenly felt very alone and very unsure. She didn't want to face the Gigglers all by herself. It seemed impossible. Then Aziza remembered everything that had happened since she'd walked through the secret fairy door and met Peri and Tiko.

'We're smart, we'll figure this out,' she said to herself. 'I'm getting that doorknob back!'

Aziza looked down at her friends one last

time, but Peri and Tiko were now just small specks and the sun was very low in the sky.

'Let my worries go,' Aziza repeated to herself as she flew high above Shimmerton's high street, chasing after the Gigglers. 'I can do it.'

With each flap of her wings, Aziza picked up speed.

I'm flying high. I'm keeping up!

Just then, the Gigglers began to slow down and Aziza couldn't quite believe it when they zoomed through a familiar storeroom window.

139

Why are we back at the toy shop? she asked

herself. What are Kendra, Felly and Noon up to

now?

The shop was dark inside with a big sign on the front door.

Shop Closed.
Mystery afoot.
Back soon.

Aziza followed the Gigglers through the window, careful not to make a noise, and ducked behind a tall shelf.

In the middle of the storeroom stood the fairies. They were surrounded by discarded toys.

'What else are you returning?' Noon asked as she rummaged through her bag.

Felly pulled out a wooden toy soldier from hers. 'I can't decide between this and the glittery keyring. I like them both.'

'Seriously, make up your minds already,' Kendra grumbled as she rubbed her left shoulder. 'I've tossed loads of toys already to make my sack lighter.'

'Perhaps we shouldn't have taken so much stuff to start with,' Felly mused. 'Even with your new special wings your sack was really heavy.

Kendra narrowed her eyes at Felly. 'Did I

ask for your opinion? Anyway, I've got the

most important thing and that's my shiny

doorknob charm,' she said, patting the bag at

her side. 'Oh, and

the marbles.'

She took

a few

out of her

bag and

examined them.

'They're so pretty.'

Felly pulled out a leftover ball of sludge and

chucked it over her shoulder. 'Yeah. I'm sure

I heard Officer Alf say they were dangerous though.'

'And something else about mind–meld marbles being difficult to control,' Noon added, twirling a pink curl around her finger.

'I wasn't listening to be honest, it was well boring,' Kendra confessed. 'Besides, did you see that Aziza girl's face when she realized we'd taken the marbles back? Classic!'

Their loud laughter filled the room and Aziza felt blood rush to her cheeks. These girls just didn't care about anyone other than themselves.

A flash of light from the marbles in Kendra's hand caught Aziza's eye.

'Hang on,' Aziza whispered to herself. 'I think it is time for a bit of mind-melding!'

She went very still as she concentrated on the twinkling lights, just like Officer Alf had said. *Come on marbles, rise up!* Aziza thought. But nothing happened.

Glittersticks! This is really hard.

Then Aziza remembered Peri's words of encouragement when she was struggling to fly.

All you need is a little practice.

Aziza closed

her eyes

and tried

to focus.

The

first marble

in Kendra's palm

twitched, then another, until all the marbles

were dancing in her hand. Kendra shrieked

and dropped them. 'They're vibrating.'

'Are they meant to do that?' Felly asked

Kendra.

Kendra shrugged. 'I don't know, do I.'

Aziza kept her focus on the marbles and
they rose from the floor, hovering in mid–air.
'Now surround the Gigglers,' she whispered.

The marbles whirled through the air and circled

Kendra, Felly and Noon at a dizzying speed.

'*Gah!* What's going on?' Kendra cried,

her arms flapping wildly.

'We're under attack,' Felly wailed as she hopped on the spot.

'I want my mummy,' said Noon.

Noon and Felly were so busy making a fuss, they barely noticed that they'd dropped their S.W.A.B. bags, or that Kendra was trying to make a run for it out of the open window still clutching hers.

But Aziza did. *Oh no you don't.* With another thought, she sent a marble whizzing into the mechanical cogs in Kendra's wings. *Gotcha!*

There was a sharp clang and suddenly

Kendra was pinging all over the place as her wings began to fail, until they finally spluttered to an abrupt halt.

'Arrgh!' Kendra yelled, but no one was listening. Her S.W.A.B. bag went flying through the air and landed on the ground with a thud. A wave of toys spilled out, including one very special, shiny jewelled doorknob.

Chapter 9

Aziza jumped out from her hiding place, quickly scooped up the doorknob and kissed it. 'Wow, am I pleased to see you!'

'I should have known you had something to do with this,' Kendra shrieked. She was currently hovering upside down. 'You ruined my lovely new wings.'

Aziza shrugged, but she did feel a bit guilty. 'Well, you shouldn't have taken all those toys or my doorknob.'

'You can keep your silly doorknob. It wouldn't have fitted on my bracelet anyway,' Kendra replied in a sulky voice.

'But you said—' Felly began.

'Oh, do be quiet,' Kendra snapped. 'There's plenty of other things we can borrow, and she can't stop us.'

Just then the storeroom door opened with

a great big *BANG* and in rushed Peri and a very angry-looking Mr Bracken.

'Right, you three,' he brayed, pointing at the Gigglers. 'Scram.'

'But ... but—' Kendra stuttered in confusion.

'No buts,' Mr Bracken broke in. 'It's very naughty taking things without permission. Even if you are just borrowing them.'

Kendra stared at him wide-eyed. 'You can't talk to us like that. We're the Gigglers.'

'We can do whatever we want,' Felly whined.

'Not in my shop, you can't,' said Mr Bracken and stamped a hoof. 'If you're not gone before I count to three, I may lose my temper, and you know what happens when a unicorn gets angry.'

'OK, OK,' Kendra said nervously. 'Let's get out of here.'

'One,' said the unicorn.

'But what about—?' Noon started to ask.

'Two,' Mr Bracken interrupted her, shaking his head. His horn flashed in the light.

'Let's go!' Kendra shrieked.

Felly and Noon rose into the air. They each grabbed hold of Kendra, whose own wings hadn't yet recovered, then off they flew out of

the window, bickering the whole way.

Aziza grinned. 'We did it, Peri! I got my

doorknob back and the Gigglers have

unborrowed the toys. But where's Tiko? He should be here to see this!'

Peri nodded her head over at Mr Bracken, and that's when Aziza noticed something strange. His nose was twitching!

I'd know that twitch anywhere, Aziza thought.

'Tiko?' she cried in amazement.

The unicorn grinned. 'Yup, I finally managed to shape-shift into something useful.'

'He was amazing,' Peri cried beside him. 'He shape-shifted into a mouse and let me into the toy shop.'

Tiko grinned excitedly. 'When we heard you arguing with the Gigglers, Peri thought we could use Mr Bracken to get them to leave.' Tiko sneezed and a cloud of sparkles surrounded him.

When it cleared, he was transformed back into his normal self. Aziza threw her arms around his neck and gave him a great big hug.

'What about me?' Peri said.

'Come here,' Aziza replied, and she pulled Peri into the huddle.

'We make a great team, don't we?' Tiko said proudly.

Peri winked at him. 'With my brilliant ideas, your shape-shifting and Aziza's super cool detective skills, we're unstoppable.'

'There's one more thing we can do as a team,' Aziza said with a laugh.

Tiko's forehead creased with a frown. 'What's that?'

'Tidy this place up.' Aziza pointed to the

toys littering the floor. 'It will be a nice thing to do for Mr Bracken.'

The three friends got to work tidying, and before long, the storeroom was back in order with everything in its place. Everything except the fairy door. It stood where Aziza left it, looking sad and flat.

'How do you know it'll work?' Peri asked.

Aziza looked down at the bejewelled doorknob in her hand. *There's only one way to find out.*

She stepped toward the fairy door and pushed the doorknob back into place. At

once, the door juddered and the painted wood shone as brightly as it had before. The edges began to shimmer and then pushed out until it was once again a proper door.

'I'm going home,' Aziza whispered. The thought made her happy and sad all at the same time. She wanted to see her family, but she was going to miss her new friends once she was back in her bedroom.

'Will you come back soon?' Tiko asked hopefully.

'Of course she will,' Peri replied breezily. 'I've just finished some homework on magic doorways at school. The door will tell you when it's time to come back, Aziza. You just need to look out for the sign.'

'Really?' Aziza let out a sigh of relief. 'I hope it's really, really soon. We're the four Fs now.'

'The four what?' Tiko asked.

'Fairy and Furry Friends Forever,' Aziza replied with a wide grin.

The three friends laughed.

With a final hug goodbye, Aziza reached for the doorknob then paused. 'What *does* happen when a unicorn loses its temper?'

'You'll have to come back and find out,'

Peri said with a wink. 'We have all sorts of magical creatures in Shimmerton. Unicorns are just the beginning.'

Aziza nodded. *I can't wait.*

'See you two soon,' she said and then opened the fairy door. Aziza stepped through and was surrounded by golden light as she entered her bedroom once more.

Aziza stared down at herself and then around her room. *Looks like I'm back to my normal size.* Her gaze moved to the windowsill and, sure enough, the fairy door was small once again, resting next to the peace lily.

Everything was quiet and the flat was still. *Everyone's asleep*, she thought. *Maybe no time passed at all while I was gone, just like a proper magical adventure.*

Aziza crept back into her bed. She had school tomorrow. 'Shame I won't be able to sleep tonight,' she whispered into the darkness. 'I'm too excited about everything that has happened.'

But soon her eyes drifted shut. After all, flying and mind-melding with marbles is awfully tiring stuff.

Myths and Legends

Aziza, her friends, and the inhabitants of Shimmerton are inspired by myths and legends from all around the world:

Aziza is named after a type of fairy creature. In West African folklore, specifically *Dahomey mythology*, the Aziza are helpful fairies who live in the forest and are full of wisdom.

Peri's name comes from ancient Persian mythology. Peris are winged spirits who can be kind and helpful, but they also sometimes enjoy playing tricks on people. In paintings they are usually shown with large, bird–like wings.

The Zorigami is based on a Japanese myth about a clock that comes to life after one hundred years.

Unicorns have appeared in folklore for thousands of years. Like Mr Bracken, they're normally portrayed as magical, horned white horses and are said to have healing powers.

Mrs Sayeed is an **Almiraj**, a legendary rabbit with a unicorn-like horn. They're found in Arabic myths and folklore.

Join Aziza on her brand new
magical adventure in

Aziza's ·Secret Fairy· 🚪 Door

and the Ice Cat Mystery

Coming in October 2021

Chapter 1

'Pass the felt tip,' Otis asked, bending over the piece of card in front of him.

Aziza stared at the jumble of coloured pens littering the dining table. 'Err, which one?'

It was the first day of the holidays and

she and her brother were busy making Jamal Justice-themed Christmas cards to send to their family.

Otis' tongue was sticking out now in concentration. 'The dark red one, I need to get JJ's cape *just* right.'

Aziza rolled her eyes. Otis was obsessed with Jamal Justice, the superhero star of the graphic novels her parents wrote and illustrated.

'Here you go.' Aziza handed him the red pen. 'Can you pass me those sequins please?'

'You can't give JJ sequins.' Otis stared at her, horrified. 'Anyway, don't you think you've made everything sparkly enough?' He looked around the room.

Aziza followed his gaze. Twinkling fairy lights and glittery tinsel hung from *every* possible surface. She loved this time of the year and felt a fizz of excitement as she thought about all the fun things her family had planned.

Glittersticks, I missed a spot, Aziza thought, spying a tinsel-free corner by the speaker. *I'll add more later. Right now, I need to finish this card for Great Aunty Az.* But something wasn't quite right. There was JJ in his superhero pose. He even had his Ray Atomizer. *So, what's missing?*

Aziza nodded to herself. *I know. I'll add Peri and Tiko.*

Her hands flew over the sheet as she drew their bodies. One had a pair of feathery wings. The other a furry face.

'Why have you put a fairy and a bear on your card?' Otis peered at Aziza's drawing.

'He's not a bear, he's a—'

'Hey Zizzles, you still helping me with the cake later?' Dad asked, popping his head through the doorway.

Otis' face creased into a disgusted frown.

He hated the Jamaican Christmas cake Dad insisted they make every year, but Aziza couldn't get enough of the sweet sticky stuff. She loved it almost as much as the spicy jollof rice mum made during the holidays.

'Yes, please!' Aziza replied. 'I just need to finish this drawin—'

'Aziza's going on about fairies again,' Otis interrupted. She's even added a fairy and a bear to her card.'

'Good stuff. Zizzles has got an amazing imagination just like her Dad.'

'And her mother,' Mum called from the kitchen.

'That's right, honey,' Dad agreed. He turned back towards Aziza and winked. 'Let me know when you're done.' Then his head disappeared again.

It didn't take long for Aziza and Otis to finish making the cards AND tidy the table. Aziza spotted a box of left over tinsel. It was crammed with all different colours. She decided that she would deal with the tinsel-free areas in the flat and then go help her dad with the cake. While Otis settled on the sofa to watch TV, Aziza set to work with the tinsel, whistling as she went.

Otis groaned. 'Cut it out, Zizi, I'm trying to watch the new episode of *Captain Bones*.'

'I'm not stopping you,' Aziza replied.

'You're whistling. *Really* loudly, and I can't see the screen past all that tinsel.'

Aziza gasped. 'But it's pretty.'

Otis rolled his eyes. 'Pretty awful you mean. And your whistling is terrible.'

'Well, that's not very nic—' she broke off as she noticed the teasing glint in Otis' eyes and realised he was just messing with her.

'I'm going to check if my room needs any more tinsel. Then I'm going to help Dad make your *favourite* cake,' Aziza announced. She started whistling again... even LOUDER and Otis' groan followed her as she left.

'Hey, Lil,' Aziza called to her peace lily as she entered her bedroom. 'You don't think my whistling is awful, do you?' She skipped past the fairy dolls and books lying on the floor and straight to the windowsill. 'Would you like some tins—'

Aziza gasped. A thin white film of frost covered the plant's glossy green leaves, and they were beginning to droop. *Oh no. What's happened?* Aziza looked around in confusion. Her room wasn't cold, and the window was definitely closed.

'What's the matter, Lil?' Aziza whispered as she bent towards the little plant. She stopped as she spotted her fairy door that always stood next to Lil. It was covered in frost too.

The metal hinges and stick-on gem door-knob glinted white, like Mum's special cookies after she dusted them with icing sugar.

Is this the sign? Aziza wondered. Peri had told her before she left Shimmerton that the fairy door would let her know when it was time to return.

A tingle went through Aziza's fingers as she reached for the tiny doorknob. The fizzy feeling spread up her hand, then through her arm as a familiar warmth filled her whole body.

'It's happening again,' Aziza breathed.

Soon she was shrinking and the glittering doorknob now filled her whole palm. It had transformed into a real jewel again. She tugged on the door, but it wouldn't budge.

Aziza frowned. *This isn't right*. She tugged

at the doorknob again, but still nothing. *It must be stiff from the frost,* she realised.

Aziza gritted her teeth and YANKED. The door swung open and a golden beam of light surrounded her. With a happy sigh, she stepped across the threshold and into the wonder beyond.

About the Authors

Lola Morayo is the pen name for the creative partnership of writers Tọ́lá Okogwu and Jasmine Richards.

Tọ́lá is a journalist and author of the Daddy Do My Hair series. She is an avid reader who enjoys spending time with her family and friends in her home in Kent, where she lives with her husband and daughters.

Jasmine is the founder of an inclusive fiction studio called Storymix and has written more than fifteen books for children. She lives in Hertfordshire with her husband and two children.

Both are passionate about telling stories that are inclusive and joyful.

About the Illustrator

© Katarina Tibenska

Cory Reid lives in Kettering and is an illustrator and designer who has worked in the creative industry for more than fifteen years with clients including, Usborne Publishing, Owlet Press and Card Factory.